OCT   1992

D0064983

Rosy Cole
Discovers America!

Books by Sheila Greenwald

Rosy Cole
Discovers America!

by Sheila Greenwald

 Little, Brown and Company
Boston   Toronto   London

For the grandparents

Copyright © 1992 by Sheila Greenwald

First Edition

The characters and events portrayed in this book are fictitious. Any similarity to real persons, living or dead, is coincidental and not intended by the author.

Library of Congress Cataloging-in-Publication Data

Greenwald, Sheila.
    Rosy Cole discovers America! / by Sheila
Greenwald. — 1st ed.
        p.   cm.
    "Joy Street Books."
    Summary: Disappointed in the poor European immigrant ancestors she discovers during a class project to research family roots, Rosy cooks up a clan of royal relatives.
    ISBN 0-316-32721-2
    [1. Genealogy — Fiction.   2. Ethnology — Fiction.   3. Schools — Fiction.]   I. Title.
PZ7.G852Ro   1992
[Fic] — dc20   92-12480

Joy Streets Books are published by
Little, Brown and Company (Inc.)

10 9 8 7 6 5 4 3 2 1

RRD-VA

Published simultaneously in Canada
by Little, Brown & Company (Canada) Limited

Printed in the United States of America

Chapter One

On the first day of school our teacher, Mrs. Oliphant, said, "Perhaps some of you remember your new class-mate from three years ago. She was here at the Read School until her family moved to California. Now we're very happy to welcome her back." Mrs. Oliphant gave the new girl a warm smile.

We all turned to look at her.

"Blaine, would you say a few words to introduce yourself to the class?" Mrs. Oliphant said.

Blaine stood up. Her face was pale and she moved her nose up and down the way a rabbit does.

"That's a tic," Mary Settleheim whispered under her breath so everyone in my row could hear.

"M-m-my name is Blaine Livingston," Blaine said.

"That's a stammer," Mary hissed.

"And I'm really g-g-glad to be back at Read."

"Since she's so g-g-glad, I wonder why she looks as if she is about to be s-sick," Mary said.

"Before you sit down, would you tell us a little about yourself?" Mrs. Oliphant asked Blaine.

"M-myself?" Blaine gasped.

"Your family," Mrs. Oliphant encouraged her. "Tell the class about your family."

From the look on her face, I figured Blaine was an orphan.

"I'm sure the class would be interested to know that your mother went to Read, and your grandmother went to Read and your great-grandmother as well."

"They would?" Blaine plopped on her seat as if her mother, grandmother, and great-grandmother had pushed her into it.

We all gave Blaine a hand.

"Thank you, Blaine," Mrs. Oliphant said. "Without knowing it, you just started our class on our special Columbus Day celebration project. Can anyone guess what it is?"

I wanted to say, "Suffering," but I kept this to myself.

A few people raised their hands.

"California?"

"The Gold Rush?"

Mrs. Oliphant shook her head. "Our Columbus Day project will help us to learn how each and every person in our class is part of a family who in their own way discovered America." She turned and wrote on the blackboard,

THE USA is US

"Usually when we begin a history project, we go to the library," Mrs. Oliphant went on, "but this time, where would you look for information?"

"Under the bed?" Debbie called out.

Everybody laughed.

"That's where we keep the box with our family's old photographs and papers," Debbie explained.

Mrs. Oliphant nodded. "Exactly. Home is where you will do your research. Ask your parents about their relatives. Write down what they tell you. Look for pictures in your photograph albums. Tomorrow we'll go around the room so you can each tell something about a relation just as Blaine has done." She held up a stack of folders. "I will give each of you a folder so you can collect your information. In two weeks, I will check what you have gathered. After that, you will select a subject from your material and begin to write a

finished report." Mrs. Oliphant wrote on the board again. *October 11.* "This is when I expect all your reports to be completed. The day after you hand them in, we will invite family and friends to a party so they can see what we have done and celebrate with us." Mrs. Oliphant spread out her arms and smiled. "We're going to find out how *all* Americans have discovered America and we're going to have wonderful fun doing it."

If Blaine was any clue, I wasn't so sure.

My name is Rosy Cole. I go to the Read School. Read is a small private school for girls on the Upper East Side of Manhattan. Until Blaine arrived I thought it was really something that my sisters, Anitra and Pippa, also went to Read. Mothers and grandmothers and great-grandmothers had never occurred to me. It never occurred to me that thinking about them would be "wonderful fun" either.

At lunch I usually sit with Hermione Wong, Linda Dildine, and Debbie Prusock. That day, when Blaine walked by our table, I pointed out an empty chair. "Would you like to eat with us?" I asked.

Her nose did a little jig. "I c-c-can't. I promised Mummy I would sit with Natalie. Her m-mummy is M-mummy's old friend. They came out together."

Blaine hopped away from our table.

"What did her mother and Natalie's mother come out of?" I asked my table.

"They came out into society, silly," Linda said. "I read all about it. There is a big fancy ball when girls turn eighteen where they get presented in beautiful dresses. They are called debutantes or debs and it's in all the newspapers."

"Why doesn't she just say, 'My mother,' like everyone else?" Debbie scrunched up her nose like Blaine's and stuck her front teeth over her lip. "I don't know her m-mummy."

"And you aren't going to," Hermione said. "Look how clicky she is."

We all turned to stare at how clicky Blaine was.

"She doesn't look clicky to me," I dis-
agreed. "She looks miserable and shy."

"Miserable and shy," Hermione hooted.
"Are those new words for stuck up and
snooty?"

"I don't think she's so bad," I informed
Hermione. I could tell Hermione was jealous. She doesn't like me to have new
friends she hasn't given the okay on.

"You and your lost causes," Hermione groaned. "Like the class rabbit nobody else would take over Easter vacation."

"You said you would train him to use the bathroom," Debbie reminded me.

"I was making real progress," I told Debbie. "Only he ate through the refrigerator cord and electrocuted himself."

"Snoupette was stupid," Hermione snapped in her most annoying and-that's-the-real-truth tone of voice. "And Blaine Livingston reminds you of him . . . and" — she wagged her finger in my face — "that's the only reason you don't think she's so bad."

I closed my eyes and shook my head. How could I explain why I wanted someone to be my friend?

I looked around the table. I liked Debbie because she was strong and sensible and I knew I could depend on her. I liked Linda because she was nervous and scared and she depended on me. I liked Kiesha because she was funny and generous. I liked Hermione because we told each other things and she never minded how embarrassing they were, and even when we had bad fights, we always ended up friends again. I liked Blaine because even though her great-granny and granny had gone to Miss Read's, she was shy. I was curious to find out what made her tick . . . and stammer, too.

"I bet you a pizza with everything on it, she is so stuck up and snooty she never invites you to her house," Hermione said.

"A pizza with everything on it," I repeated. "It's a bet."

16

At dinner I told my parents about Blaine.

"I remember the Livingstons from when you were in first grade," Mom said. "They are a very old family."

"Do they all have beards and canes?" I tried to picture it.

Mom shook her head. "Old family means they have been in this country for generations and can trace their ancestors who were famous and powerful in American society."

"What about us?" I asked. I thought of our "USA is US" Columbus Day project. "Can we trace our ancestors?"

"All we know about the Coles and the Popkins is that a hundred years ago, life in the old country was so hard they wanted to get out of it."

"Where was the old country?"

"Ireland, Wales, Sweden, and Denmark for me," Dad said.

"Poland, Hungary, Austria, and Russia for me," Mom said.

"What was so hard about it?" I asked.

"My great-granny Cole was escaping the potato famine in Ireland," Dad said. "Mom's great-granny was fleeing the pogroms in Eastern Europe."

"A famine means they were starving, and a pogrom means they were being attacked," Mom added, just in case I thought they were something good.

"Wasn't anybody famous?" I asked.

"Somebody once told me that Great-great-uncle Joseph was a famous horse thief." Mom laughed.

This was not the kind of famous I wanted to stand up and tell my class about.

WANTED
HORSE THIEF
ROSY'S
UNCLE
JOSEPH

"Sorry, Rosy," Mom said. "We are not an old, established American family. All our great-grandparents were hardworking immigrants who came to this country with little money and big dreams."

I had a funny feeling that at Miss Read's School, old family was better than new, and big money better than big dreams.

"Cheer up," my father said. "Even though none of your great-great-grannies would have been accepted in the Read School, America is such a wonderful country, their children and children's children, like you, have had the opportunity to be whoever they want to be and to go to a school like Miss Read's."

What was there to cheer up about? A great-great-granny who couldn't have set foot inside my school?

Right now I wished to be a person with a great-great-granny with the right feet.

Chapter Two

The next morning, Mrs. Oliphant stood in front of the blackboard with the words *The USA is US* on it. She called on Natalie Pringle. "Natalie, can you tell the class about a great-great-grandparent or -uncle or -aunt?"

"My great-aunt Fiona was famous for her beauty. All the men were in love with her," Natalie gushed. "She was the most beautiful debutante of her season. She came out at the New York Assemblies and also was presented to the queen at the Court of Saint James's. She married Lord Betteson, the great yachtsman, and she settled in England."

"Wonderful." Mrs. Oliphant smiled from ear to ear. "What grand good times they must have had." You could almost see her waving Great-aunt Fiona off on a cruise.

I tried to picture her waving Great-great-uncle Joseph off on a stolen horse. I couldn't.

After Natalie it was Debbie's turn. "My great-great-grandpa escaped from Russia in a laundry basket to avoid being taken into the tsar's army," she said.

"A frightening journey, I'm sure." Mrs. Oliphant's voice grew serious at the thought. "Full of sacrifice and courage."

That was when I saw Mary Settleheim make a face at Natalie Pringle and say, "Ugh."

The next person Mrs. Oliphant called on was Keisha.

"My family came from Africa on slave ships," she said.

"What stories of suffering and loss they could tell." Mrs. Oliphant shook her head sadly. "What a painful chapter in American history."

That was when I saw Mary Settleheim make a face at Jenny Gilchrist, and heard Jenny Gilchrist say, "Ychh."

That was when I knew my funny feeling the night before was right. At Miss Read's School it was better to tell about yachts and coming-out balls than slave ships and laundry baskets.

By the time Mrs. Oliphant called on me, I was ready. "I had a great-great-uncle Joseph who was famous for horses," I said.

"And where was that?" Mrs. Oliphant asked.

"Austria, Hungary," I said.

"Oh my." She grinned. "An Austro-Hungarian Equestrian. How romantic." The way she put it, it sounded even better than I'd hoped. Mrs. Oliphant wanted more information, but I told her I needed to do some research. In the meantime, I knew I was on the right track. Nobody said, "Ugh," or "Ychh," or rolled her eyes.

Hermione grabbed my arm as soon as class was over. "Where did you get that uncle from, Rosy?" she asked suspiciously.

"Home," I said, taking a step back.

"Whose?" Hermione took a step closer.

"Mine." I took another step back.

Blaine stepped between us. "My great-uncle Fredrick had horses, too," she said to me. "They were Arabians. What did your uncle ride, Rosy?"

"I think they were Egyptians," I said. "Or maybe Italians. I'll have to check."

"They sound more like Imaginaries to me," Hermione muttered.

"I would love to see a picture of your uncle Fredrick's horse," I told Blaine. "Or anything else you have a picture of." I figured I could probably learn everything I needed to know about old families just by walking around her living room.

"Not today," Blaine said, shaking her head. "I have a date with Mary." She waved to Mary over my shoulder. "We want to show Mary the photos of her m-mummy and mine from when they were b-both at the Read School."

"I can't make it, Blaine," Mary called out. "I forgot to tell you, I have to go to the orthodontist."

"Y-yesterday you said you could come," Blaine wailed. "We b-baked G-great-g-grandma Eliot's oatmeal cookies specially for you."

"I couldn't eat them anyway." Mary shuddered. "They'd stick in my braces." She hurried away, as if any minute Blaine would stick in her braces, too.

"Why don't you invite someone to your house who has no braces?" I suggested to Blaine.

I smiled so she would know who.

As soon as we got to Blaine's, her mother introduced herself to me. "If there's anything you'd like, please help yourself, Rosy." She pointed to the round table in the kitchen where there was a

plate of cookies and a pitcher of apple
juice. "The cookies are Great-gran Eliot's
original recipe for Yankee oatmeal."

At Blaine's house I ate lots of old family
cookies and saw plenty of old family, too.

"Who's that?" I asked Blaine.

"D-do you really want to know?"

Blaine got red in the face.

"Blainey dear," Mrs. Livingston said. "Why don't you tell your new friend about the portraits?"

Blaine sighed and began to recite. "This is my great-great-great-great-great-uncle Fredrick. King Charles the Second of England gave him twenty miles upstate. I think he was governor or senator or something." She pointed to the portrait next to it. "That's Great-great-great-uncle Tobias Matheson. He was on the Supreme Court and the first president of City College. The painting is a copy because we gave the original to the Museum of the City of New York. He was married to Alma Van Alan, who was a great beauty. She was from Van Alansville. The Matheson side of the family is all from Mathesonport."

"Where do your people come from, Rosy?" Mrs. Livingston asked me.

"Coleport," I said, before I had time to think. "And the Popkins are from Popkinville, which is out West someplace." I figured if you went far enough west you eventually got to Austria, Hungary, Poland, and Russia and maybe a place called Popkinville.

"What fun," Mrs. Livingston said. "To have a whole town with your name on it."

Next, Mrs. Livingston got out her old yearbook from Read. "Here's Mary Settleheim's mummy and Natalie's aunt Tessa. Isn't it too sweet? We all came out together. That's what I love about Read. It's like family."

It wasn't like *my* family. There was no way I'd find my mother in an old Read yearbook unless I stuck her there with rubber cement.

After that, we went to Blaine's room and she showed me her collection of dolls. "They have been passed down from one generation of my family to the next," she said. "M-my mother calls them heirlooms, but to me they are like old friends who have a history and I love them."

"I know just what you mean," I agreed. "I love my old dolls, too." I wasn't lying. I did love my old dolls, even if they had never been anybody else's old dolls.

"My old dolls don't hurt my feelings the way Mary did," Blaine said.

"Mary is hard on new people," I explained. "She teases so nobody will tease her first."

"I only asked her over because my m-mother wants me to be with people who are related to her friends." Blaine sighed. "It never works out. They don't like me and I don't like them." She smiled. "But you're different, Rosy. My mother didn't tell me to pick you out. *I* picked you and you picked me. We picked each other. That makes us friends."

"Yes, it does," I agreed. How could I ever explain this to Hermione?

When it was time to leave, Blaine and her mother walked me to the door.

"It was nice to meet you," Mrs. Livingston said. "I hope you will visit soon again."

I was so excited I practically ran all the way home.

I had seen an old family and made a new friend. And if that weren't enough, I would soon eat a pizza with everything on it.

Chapter Three

That night at dinner, I told my family about our school project for Columbus Day, "The USA is US."

My mother got all excited. "You could write about Great-granny Popkin. Her ship sunk in the Atlantic and she floated around in a lifeboat until she was picked up."

"What picked her up?"

I was praying for a yacht.

"One of those large steamers like the one she started out on, jammed into steerage class with all the other poor immigrants," Mom said.

I could just hear Mary's "Ugh," and Jenny's "Ychh." I tried another subject. "Do we have any family heirlooms?"

"There are the brass candlesticks from Grandma Cole and the teapot from Great-grandma Popkin."

"What about portraits? Where are the pictures of our ancestors?"

Dad found an old photo album that was practically falling apart. "Is this what you want?" he said, handing it to me.

It certainly wasn't.

But I flipped through the pages anyway. There was no sign of the kind of relative I had seen on Blaine's wall. "Was anybody a debutante?" I asked.

My mother began to laugh. "Coming out is only for wealthy and privileged young women, Rosy. Just look at those photographs. Do you think anybody in them ever got presented to society at a fancy debutante ball?"

I had to admit that it didn't seem likely.

"Lena and Fanny didn't 'come out,' but they went to night school so they could learn to speak English better. Lena became a social worker. Great-granny Cole took in boarders to help support her three sons and two daughters. She started an amateur singing society." Dad turned the pages of the album. "You won't find the names of privileged and powerful people here," he said. "But look." He pointed to the last picture in the album. It was all my aunts and uncles and cousins at a picnic.

"You have a large, loving, and living family," Dad said. "No portraits on the wall or heirlooms on the shelf can compare to them in value."

I examined the picture. Not one of my relatives was a college president or a Supreme Court judge. Nobody was given land by a king. Nobody ever came out. I loved them, but I couldn't use them in my folder.

As soon as dinner was over, I called Hermione to tell her about my visit to Blaine's.

"Now that you've eaten Great-granny Eliot's Original Recipe Yankee Oatmeal Cookies, maybe you're not interested in pizza," she said.

"No such luck. I'll start saving up my appetite."

"I'll start saving up my allowance," Hermione grumbled.

In the morning, Blaine was waiting for me in the locker room. "When can I visit your house, Rosy?" she asked me. "I would love to see your heirloom doll collection."

"Heirloom doll collection?" Hermione-Big-Ears grinned. "You mean that bald Raggedy Ann that Pippa threw out and you saved from the garbage?"

"I mean the really old dolls from my great-great-granny that I am not allowed to play with except when I am by myself," I said very slowly, avoiding Hermione's glare.

"Can I visit next Monday?" Blaine asked. "M-mummy says it's okay with her."

It might have been okay with Mummy but it was bad news for me. I had less than a week to come up with heirloom dolls and something to put in my "USA is US" folder.

When I got home from school, I counted

up the days I had to get ready for Blaine's
visit.

I had a lot to do. First I polished the
brass candlesticks and the silver-plated
teapot.

Then I tried a few relatives on the wall.

I was able to make some improvement with scissors and tape, but Great-great-uncle Joseph the Austro-Hungarian Equestrian was still a problem.

"Rosy, what has come over you?" Mom asked me.

"It's part of our school project," I said.

"But you're turning our apartment into a museum." She laughed.

"That's *it!*" I cried. And I gave my mother a big kiss for giving me just the idea I needed for Blaine's visit.

On the morning of Blaine's visit, I added some finishing touches.

"How long do we have to live like this?" Mom asked.

"Just till this afternoon," I promised her.

Since Hermione lives in my building, she walked home from school with Blaine and me. "I have delicious almond cookies my aunt Dylice gave us," Hermione said. "I could bring them over."

"No thanks," I said. "We have Great-granny Isabel's Classic Fudge Brownies."

"You can always use more cookies," Hermione insisted.

"I am allergic to nuts," I told her. "Especially almonds."

When Hermione got off the elevator at her floor, she looked as if she had suddenly developed an allergy, too.

As it turned out there were nuts in Great-granny Isabel's Classic Fudge Brownies and Blaine said she was allergic to chocolate.

"That's okay," Blaine said. "I always bring my own snack." She opened her plastic bag of carrot sticks. I hated to admit it, but Hermione was right. She

really did remind me of Snoupette.

After she finished munching, she wiped her lips with a little cloth napkin she pulled out of her knapsack.

"Would you like to see our collection?" I asked.

"What do you collect?" Blaine asked.

"Family treasures," I said. "The ones we haven't given away to the Museum of the City of New York."

"Your family donated to the museum, too?" Blaine asked excitedly. I could see how happy she was that we had something in common.

"Come see the little teapot and the candlesticks we kept to remind us of the past."

I took Blaine to the dining room and showed her our treasures.

"Why did your family give so much away?" she asked.

"M-mummy hates clutter." Suddenly I began to stutter just like Blaine.

"What about clothes? Did you keep any of the old gowns?"

"Oh yes," I could feel myself really getting into it. "For instance the dress my great-great-grandmother wore to her coming-out party."

"How fantastic!" Blaine clapped her hands. "We saved those dresses, too. Wouldn't it be fun to put them on sometime and wear them to a party?"

"It would be wonderful," I agreed. "Only the dress is in storage and there isn't any party I could wear it to." Sometimes I think so fast I amaze even myself.

"But there is!" Blaine began to jump up and down with excitement. "We could wear them to the Columbus Day 'USA is US' celebration party at school! Everybody can come dressed as her great-great-grandmother. That way we could see how they might have looked. Oh, Rosy, this idea is so much fun, I could p-practically faint."

That made two of us. Inventing a great-granny was easy. Finding her a real ball gown wasn't.

Chapter Four

Monday morning I put my folder on Mrs. Oliphant's desk.

"What do you call this, Rosy?" she asked. "It's empty."

"Everything is out on loan," I explained. "But it will all be returned by the time I need to write my report."

"I certainly hope so." Mrs. Oliphant handed it back.

When the folders had been collected, Blaine raised her hand. "I had the idea that we could all dress up like our great-great-grannies for the 'USA is US' celebration on Columbus Day," she said without a stammer.

"What a wonderful idea," Mrs. Oliphant congratulated Blaine. "Then you could each tell something about the dresses and the women who wore them."

Right away, I could see Blaine's idea had really caught on with some people

but not with others.

At lunch Jenny was all excited. "I'm going to wear the same dress my great-great-granny wore to have her portrait painted by Sinclair."

Everyone at Jenny's table told her they couldn't wait to see her dress.

At my table, Debbie leaned over her tray and groaned. "My mother told me my great-great-granny came here with nothing but dreams. Is that what I'm supposed to wear?"

Keisha turned around in her seat. "I have no idea what my great-great-granny wore," she told Blaine.

"Why don't you just look at some old p-portraits?" Blaine suggested.

"That's right, everybody has some of them," Mary Settleheim joined in.

"Not everybody who came from Africa on a slave ship," Keisha said under her breath.

"Not everybody who escaped Russia in a laundry basket," Debbie said.

"Not everybody who left China on a fishing boat," Hermione added.

51

"Oh, I forgot." Blaine looked upset.

"It's easy to forget," Mary said. "People like that never went to Miss Read's."

I remembered my father had said people like Great-great-granny Popkin couldn't have set foot inside Miss Read's School. I could just imagine what Mary would say if she found out about Great-great-granny Popkin.

On the way home from school, Hermione said, "What will you wear to the 'USA is US' celebration, Rosy? One of your great-great-granny's fancy ball gowns?"

"How did you guess?" I answered as if she weren't teasing.

Hermione just looked at me, so I knew

more was coming. "In all the years I've
known you, Rosy, you never once said a
single word about this great-great-granny
who went to balls or that great-uncle who
rode horses. How come?"

"I didn't want to make you jealous," I
said quickly.

Hermione was amazed. "Why would I
be jealous, when I have Great-grandpa
Wong?"

"Was he important and famous in
China?"

"He was poor and miserable," Hermione
said. "He came here to make a better life.
America gave him the chance he wanted.
If you come up to my place, I can show

you a picture of Great-grandpa Wong standing in the doorway of his very first laundry. You know Chinese people went into the laundry business because they weren't allowed to do other kinds of work. But my relatives made the best of the situation."

Hermione looked as if she were about to burst with pride.

What was she so proud of? Making the best of misery and poverty? Misery and poverty weren't fame and wealth. Even if you made the best of them, they were nothing to be proud of. I shook my head and told her I would see the photo some other time. I had to go home and locate Great-great-granny Popkin's ball gown so I could wear it to the "USA is US" party.

Before I even opened the door to my apartment, I smelled strange odors.

In the kitchen were my sisters and my parents and my aunt Sylvia.

"Hello, sweetheart." Aunt Sylvia gave me a big, wet kiss. "Thanks a zillion for a great party idea."

I didn't know what she was talking about, so my mother explained.

"When Aunt Sylvia heard you were asking questions about the family, she came up with a wonderful plan for a reunion."

"We're cooking Great-granny Popkin's favorite dishes." Aunt Sylvia pointed to the pots on the stove. "And we're going to invite everybody we can find. Including the last two cousins to come from the old country, Zadie and Mushi."

"What are they like?" I asked.

"You'll see," Mom said in a tone that sometimes meant, "You'll see something you may not want to see."

"What are you cooking?" I thought the pots on the stove were a safer subject than Zadie and Mushi.

"Peasant cabbage soup." Aunt Sylvia stirred the pot. "Nothing fancy, but good and nourishing and honest, just like Zadie and Mushi." She tasted a spoonful. "We're preparing it now so we can pop it in the freezer and take it out when it's time for the party."

"Will freezing take away the strong smell?"

"Who knows? It's from Great-granny Popkin's recipe. She didn't have a freezer. She didn't even have a refrigerator."

"But she sure had a strong garlic smell." Mom laughed.

"Blaine's great-great-granny had a recipe for Yankee oatmeal cookies," I said.

"Why don't you invite Blaine to our party?" Mom suggested. "It would be a new experience for her."

For me, too. Nightmaresville. I couldn't think of anything worse.

My mother gave me a head of cabbage to shred. "You could put the recipe for this

soup in that folder you have for your 'USA is US' Columbus Day project," she said.

I was beginning to be sorry I had told her about my folder.

"You must put in how your great-great-granny Popkin's ship broke down and she had to be rescued from a lifeboat," Aunt Sylvia said.

"Was she the great-great-granny who was such a wonderful seamstress?" my sister Anitra asked.

"Yes," Mom nodded. "The foreman of the sweatshop where she worked noticed her perfect tiny stitches right away, and he turned out to be your great-great-grandpa Popkin."

"He must have noticed more than her perfect tiny stitches," Pippa said, and giggled.

"Did she sew party clothes and ball gowns?" I held my breath. Maybe this would be my lucky day after all.

"Let's take a look in the album, and see what she's wearing," my mother suggested.

Pippa squinted at the photo. "She sewed them, but she certainly didn't wear them."

"Her life was hard." Aunt Sylvia sighed. "Even though she knew how to make the best of her situation. Can you imagine how it felt to leave your family and village and set out with practically no money to a new land where you didn't even understand the language?"

No. I couldn't imagine it, and I didn't want to. If I was going to imagine something, it was a great-great-granny who sailed on yachts and had beautiful clothes and went to wonderful balls. My family stories and my family photographs were no help.

I would have to look in another place to find something for my folder.

And I knew exactly what that place would be.

Chapter Five

The next morning, as soon as I got to school, I hurried to the library.

"What is it, Rosy?" Mrs. Medoff asked.

"Old Families, Old Money, Old New York," I said. "Parties and balls."

Mrs. Medoff found me a large book. It had everything.

ARRIVING
At THE BALL

THE OPERA

THE BALL
SUPPER

I made copies of the pictures for my folder, and when I got home I looked in my closet to see if I could find the clothes my great-great-granny would have worn.

High neck with lace? It was right there in my nighties drawer.

High heels?
They were in Anitra's closet.

All I needed were a few ribbons and a bow or two and a couple of strings of pearls from Mom's room, and I was all set.

It wasn't as if I was making up anything. I was just helping my relatives be the people they wanted to be... Americans.

The phone rang. It was Blaine. "Could you come visit me tomorrow after school, Rosy?" she asked. "We could play with the dolls."

"Not tomorrow," I said. "I have to start work on my 'USA is US' report."

"What's your topic?" Blaine asked.

I looked at my reflection in the mirror and saw my topic right in front of me.

"My Great-great-granny Popkin's Parties," I said.

"Oh, tell me about them."

"There was one where everybody came on horseback. The guests ate off silver plates with gold forks while they sat on their horses." I remembered the picture of that party in the book Mrs. Medoff gave me.

"Will you wear the dress she wore to the Horseback Ball?"

"Either that one or the one she wore to the Opera Ball," I said, really getting into it. "She went to tons of balls."

"Oh, R-rosy, what fun. Isn't this the most wonderful f-fun?"

"It certainly is," I agreed. I was going to have my great-great-granny Popkin go to every single ball in the book.

Writing my report on Great-great-granny Popkin was so exciting, I couldn't wait to start work on it every day when I came home from school.

I used everything I could think of in my writing.

GRANDMA POPKIN

Scotch tape and scissors and photographs and rubber cement.

GRANNY POPKIN AT THE BALL SUPPER

All the while I was preparing my report, my mother and Aunt Sylvia were preparing for the family reunion.

"Don't forget the family reunion," my mother said. She made a big circle on my calendar. "I want you to come home right after school, so you can give me a hand."

"But it's the same day we have to turn in our 'USA is US' reports," I said.

"Then you'll feel like celebrating. Perhaps some of your classmates would like to come to our party, too. We'll have plenty of good food and company."

Peasant Cabbage Soup? Zadie and Mushi? "No thanks," I told my mother.

"Too bad," she said. "They would have fun."

Mainly, I thought, they would *make* fun . . . of me.

Every time I looked at the red circle my mother had drawn on my calendar, it gave me a sick feeling.

It took me two whole weeks to finish my report. It was ready one whole day before it was due. I put it on top of my desk and went off to school. I felt like celebrating.

"You never bought me that pizza with everything on it," I reminded Hermione on the way home from school.

She counted the money in her change purse. "A bet is a bet," she grumbled, as if she wished it weren't.

"This bet wasn't hard to win," I said. "Blaine invited me to her house because she likes me and because we have so much in common."

"You mean those uncles who ride on horses?" Hermione snickered. "I'll believe that Hungarian Equestrian when I see him, or his picture." She pushed open the door to Vinnie's Pizzeria and marched up to the counter as if she had already spotted my great-great-uncle Joseph stealing a horse.

"What'll it be?" Vinnie asked.

All of a sudden I remembered I had no picture of Uncle Joseph or his horse. "I'll eat pizza some other time," I said to Hermione, and before she could ask me any questions, I ran out of Vinnie's.

69

I got back to our school just as Mrs. Medoff was closing the library. "Austro-Hungarian Anything," I panted.

She found me a nice big book full of pictures and maps.

There was something called the Austro-Hungarian Empire.

It had someone called Franz Joseph for an emperor . . . and he

Emperor Franz Joseph
uncle

rode a horse.
Why not?

    I made a copy of the picture to put in my report as soon as I got home.
    Now I was really ready.

Chapter Six

The next morning Mrs. Oliphant collected our reports. "Tomorrow I will put all these reports into a big loose-leaf book." She showed us the book. On the cover of the book she had stuck a printed label which read:

THE
USA IS US
BY
The Student's
of
Mrs. Oliphant's
Class

"In this book we have history," Mrs. Oliphant said as she opened the first report. "Here is the story of Great-grandpa Wong." She held up Hermione's report so we could see the photograph of a small Chinese man standing in the doorway of a laundry. Mrs. Oliphant began to read about how Mr. Wong came to America alone and worked to bring over his wife and children. They experienced many hardships, but they were able to open their own business and send all their children through school so that they could have the careers they wished for.

Mrs. Oliphant picked up another report.

"Here is Michael McCurry. He helped build the railroads that would connect our great country from coast to coast." She showed us a picture of Christi's great-great-grandfather standing by a railroad track with a huge hammer in his hand.

"And here is Debbie's great-great-grandmother, who helped to organize the workers at the sweatshop where she sewed so they could have better conditions. She was part of the very beginning of the labor movement that spread throughout our country." We all tried to get a look at Debbie's great-great-grandmother.

It was exciting to see an actual person who had worked hard to make an important change in our country. She had a strong and serious face. Debbie was bursting with pride.

"And here is Blaine's great-great-great-uncle who was the president of City College where young people without money could earn an education . . . and . . ." Mrs. Oliphant turned another page. . . . "Here is Rosy's great-great-granny Popkin who . . .

went to parties and was

directly related to the Emperor ... Franz Joseph of ...?" Mrs. Oliphant began to choke, so she stopped reading and just held up the page with all my pictures.

Nobody said, "Ychh," or "Ugh," but Mrs. Oliphant said, "Rosy, I would like to see you for a moment before you go home today."

Then she read about Natalie's great-great-aunt Lavinia who was a suffragette, which meant she fought for a woman's right to vote.

Mrs. Oliphant went on and on. She was making it sound as if everybody's relatives had done something wonderful to make America great. Jenny's great-great-granny who collected paintings and left them to the museum, and Keisha's great-great-great-granny who was a slave and escaped to the North during the Civil War and started a school in Philadelphia to teach black children to read and write.

When she was finished going through the reports, Mrs. Oliphant said, "Tomorrow is our Columbus Day 'USA is US' party. Tell your parents and friends they are welcome to come."

She left our reports on her desk so that we could take turns looking through them before they went into the loose-leaf binder. I stood back to make room for the line that would form in front of my report.

It wasn't necessary.

I had worked so hard to put my great-great-granny in the best clothes and send her to the best parties. What was wrong with her? What did I leave out?

As soon as the bell rang, I grabbed my coat and ran for it. Mrs. Oliphant motioned to me to stay.

"I'm late for my family reunion," I called to her, and was through the door before she could stop me.

When I got home from school, our apartment was already filling up with relatives.

There were Aunt Sylvia and Uncle Charlie. My three cousins from New Jersey and five more from Massachusetts. There were Uncle Ralph and Aunt Teddy and a bunch of second cousins from Pennsylvania. Somebody flew in from Chicago and somebody else came all the way from Seattle. There were old people and babies. There were relatives I knew and relatives I had never met before.

All of a sudden the doorbell rang and there were Zadie and Mushi.

When they walked into the room, the whole party stopped eating and drinking and laughing and talking.

Here's what happened next.

Everyone hugged Zadie and Mushi.

Zadie and Mushi hugged everyone.

Everyone got Zadie and Mushi plates of food and asked them to sit down.

Everyone asked Zadie and Mushi questions.

Zadie began.

"We waited so long to get permission to come to America, maybe it was easier for Great-granny Popkin, who was only poor and struggling without a nickel to her name and had to make a trip in miserable steerage on a ship that broke down. At least she didn't have to worry about being punished and losing her job and ending up in prison."

"How did you keep your spirits up?" Mom asked.

"Sometimes we sang songs," Mushi said.

"What kind of songs?" Aunt Teddy called out.

Zadie closed her eyes and swayed her head back and forth. Then she began to sing. Even though I couldn't understand the words, the song made me feel how sad and lost the person was who sang it.

Aunt Sylvia cried out, "Grandma used to sing that song. It's about a mother too poor to feed her child." She joined in the chorus. So did my mother and Uncle Ralph and Aunt Teddy and then everybody else began to sing. If they didn't know the words, they hummed.

When the song ended, Zadie's cheeks were wet with tears. Mushi stood up. "Enough tears," she said, and she began to clap her hands. "Time for a happy song."

"How about this?" Teddy sat down at the piano and started playing.

Mushi took Zadie around the waist and Mom took Mushi and Ralph grabbed Mom.

My cousin Eddie grabbed me by the hand and pulled me into the circle. Before I knew it, I was dancing, too!

And in minutes there was a whole circle of people dancing around our living room while Aunt Teddy played the piano faster and faster.

Maybe this was not old family, but this was MY family and I loved it . . .

and the very next day, I was going to stand up in front of my class and pretend it didn't even exist.

How could I?

I couldn't.

What would I do?

I had to think of something.

Chapter Seven

Our party went on until nearly nine o'clock at night.

After everyone left, we tidied up and I got ready for bed. My great-great-granny's ball gown hung on the door of my closet.

I tried to fall asleep, but the ball gown kept me awake even when I closed my eyes.

I took it down from the closet door and put it in the bathroom. But that didn't work.

How could I go to school and be in the "USA is US" celebration in that dress?

How could I stand up in front of my parents in that dress?

I put my head under the water tap to wash the nightgown thoughts out of it . . .

and then I knew what I had to do.

I dried my head, climbed back into bed, and went to sleep.

In the morning, I got dressed. My parents were still asleep. They had been up late after our party. In the kitchen Pippa and Anitra stared at me.

"What do you call that?" Pippa asked me.

"A look," I said. "I have a few more things to do with it."

"I can't imagine what." Anitra rolled her eyes.

"I'll bet you can't," I said, and I really had to laugh.

After breakfast, I put on my jacket and waved good-bye.

In the lobby of my building, Eddie, the doorman, handed me a note from Hermione.

To Her Royal Highness
The Empress   Rosy-
    I couldn't wait
                Hermione
                Wong

By the time I got to school, Mrs. Oliphant had set up our classroom. She had put a table in the corner under a window. On the table there were paper plates and bowls of food that some people had brought from home. There was a big pitcher of apple juice. In the middle of the table was the loose-leaf book that held all our reports. Parents were gathered around the book taking turns looking at it. Some of them were sipping from the paper cups or munching on Blaine's oatmeal cookies or Hermione's egg rolls or Linda's kasha varnishkes.

Mrs. Oliphant went to her desk. "Welcome everyone," she said. "Thank you for joining us in our celebration of Columbus Day and 'The USA is US.' Won't you all please take a seat?"

While the parents sat down, Mrs. Oliphant asked our class to stand in a line in front of the room.

"The students had a wonderful idea to dress as their great-great-grandmothers for this party," Mrs. Oliphant said. "I thought it would be interesting for each of them to tell us something about the dress she is wearing and about its original owner."

Jenny Gilchrist was first. "This is the very same dress my great-great-granny wore to have her portrait painted by the artist Thomas Sinclair," Jenny said, while the parents craned their necks to get a really good look at her dress. "Every bit of this dress was made by hand. Just look at the teensy, tiny stitches." Jenny turned up

the hem of her dress so everyone could see what she was talking about. While everybody was examining Jenny's dress, I left the room by the front door just as my parents were entering it by the back door. Following my parents were Zadie and Mushi.

They didn't see me. I ran down the hall

to the bathroom to put the final touches
onto my costume.

BATHROOM

Finally I was ready
to go back to Mrs.
Oliphant's room.

"Rosy Cole," Mrs. Oliphant
gasped, "you're sopping wet."

"That's because my great-great-granny's
ship went down," I said. "She had to float
around in a lifeboat till she was rescued."

"Did she drown?" Mary asked.

"No, she landed in New York and
worked as a seamstress in a sweatshop.
Her work was very fine." I pointed to the
hem of Jenny's dress. "Maybe she even
sewed those teensy, tiny stitches. Her sew-
ing was admired by the foreman and he
married her."

"This story is even better than the Horseback Ball," Blaine said, clapping.

"This story is true," I said. "I made up fancy balls for my great-great-granny so you would think I had a real old American family and that would give us something in common."

Everyone was quiet.

"We *do* have something in common," Blaine said. "We like each other."

I looked over at my parents and Zadie and Mushi. "I made up stories about Great-great-granny Popkin so nobody would say, 'Ugh,' and 'Ychh,' and 'People like that never went to Miss Read's.' I was ashamed of my family until I got more ashamed of being ashamed."

"But wait a m-minute," Blaine stammered. "We aren't our great-great-grannies."

"Exactly." Mrs. Oliphant put her hand on my shoulder and beamed at me as if she had planned all along for me to stand up in front of an audience in a dripping wet nightgown confessing that I had been ashamed of my family.

"We are different from our great-great-grannies and our great-great-grannies were different from one another. We are different from one another, too," Mrs. Oliphant went on. "But whether our people came here two hundred years ago or two days ago, it is these differences that have made our country strong and great."

Nobody said anything, and then Hermione grinned and began to clap.

Everyone else began to clap, too, as if we were part of a Columbus Day skit about how someone named Rosy Cole discovered an America where it didn't matter if your family was new or old or rich or poor . . . we were all part of it. The USA WAS US!

Since everybody was clapping their hands and looking at me . . .

I took a bow. Why not?

I was making the best of my situation, just like Great-great-granny Popkin had a long time ago.

And besides, I had just discovered America, hadn't I?